Shake a Leg, EGG!

Shake a Leg, EGG!

Kurt Cyrus

Beach Lane Books • New York   London   Toronto   Sydney   New Delhi

Hello in there!
Are you aware . . .

how long we've all
been waiting?

Coots are circling.
Nosy crows are calling and debating.

What's the holdup?
No one knows.

We're waiting, waiting, waiting!

Buds are bursting open.

Sprouts are breaking through.

Eggs are hatching everywhere.

You can do it too!

All around you, life is brimming,

swimming, slapping, honking, flapping.

Conversations fill the air.
Don't *you* have a peep to share?

Wings are whistling
overhead.
Up they rise!
Off they fly!
Soon you too
will cross the sky.

For where does every flight begin?

A nest. An egg. A chick like you,
who picks and pecks and . . .

pokes on through!

Meet the pond.
Greet the sun.
Say hello to everyone!

The whole wide world is waiting.

To Andrea
and her hatchling, Anna

BEACH LANE BOOKS • An imprint of Simon & Schuster Children's Publishing Division • 1230 Avenue of the Americas, New York, New York 10020 • Copyright © 2017 by Kurt Cyrus • All rights reserved, including the right of reproduction in whole or in part in any form. • BEACH LANE BOOKS is a trademark of Simon & Schuster, Inc. • For information about special discounts for bulk purchases, please contact Simon & Schuster Special Sales at 1-866-506-1949 or business@simonandschuster.com. • The Simon & Schuster Speakers Bureau can bring authors to your live event. For more information or to book an event, contact the Simon & Schuster Speakers Bureau at 1-866-248-3049 or visit our website at www.simonspeakers.com. • Book design by Lauren Rille • The text for this book was set in Slimtype. • Manufactured in China • 1216 SCP • First Edition • 10 9 8 7 6 5 4 3 2 1 • Library of Congress Cataloging-in-Publication Data • Names: Cyrus, Kurt, author. • Title: Shake a leg, egg! / Kurt Cyrus. • Description: First Edition. | New York : Beach Lane Books, 2017. | Summary: "It's springtime, and the pond is bursting with new life. There are beaver pups, heron hatchlings, and lots and lots of ducklings. Everyone is out and about, swimming, flapping, chirping, and quacking—except for one family of geese"—Provided by publisher. • Identifiers: LCCN 2016018823 | ISBN 9781481458481 (hardback) | ISBN 9781481458498 (eBook) • Subjects: | CYAC: Stories in rhyme. | Geese—Fiction. | Spring—Fiction. | Animals—Infancy—Fiction. | Humorous stories. | BISAC: JUVENILE FICTION / Animals / Ducks, Geese, etc. | JUVENILE FICTION / Family / New Baby. • Classification: LCC PZ8.3.C997 Sh 2017 | DDC [E]—dc23 LC record available at https://lccn.loc.gov/2016018823